Following Magic

Read all the books in the
Faeries' Promise series:

Silence and Stone

The Faeries' Promise
Following Magic

BY KATHLEEN DUEY

Illustrated by
SANDARA TANG

Aladdin
New York   London   Toronto   Sydney

For Ellen Krieger, with love and thanks . . .

This book is a work of fiction. Any references to historical events, real people, or real locales are used fictitiously. Other names, characters, places, and incidents are the product of the author's imagination, and any resemblance to actual events or locales or persons, living or dead, is entirely coincidental.

ALADDIN
An imprint of Simon & Schuster Children's Publishing Division
1230 Avenue of the Americas, New York, NY 10020
First Aladdin paperback edition November 2010
Text copyright © 2010 by Kathleen Duey
Illustrations copyright © 2010 by Sandara Tang
All rights reserved, including the right of reproduction in whole or in part in any form.
ALADDIN is a trademark of Simon & Schuster, Inc., and related logo is a registered trademark of Simon & Schuster, Inc.
Also available in an Aladdin hardcover edition.
For information about special discounts for bulk purchases, please contact Simon & Schuster Special Sales at 1-866-506-1949 or business@simonandschuster.com.
The Simon & Schuster Speakers Bureau can bring authors to your live event. For more information or to book an event contact the Simon & Schuster Speakers Bureau at 1-866-248-3049 or visit our website at www.simonspeakers.com.
Designed by Lisa Vega
The text of this book was set in Adobe Garamond.
The illustrations for this book were rendered digitally.
Manufactured in the United States of America 1010 OFF
2 4 6 8 10 9 7 5 3 1
The Library of Congress has cataloged the hardcover edition as follows:
Duey, Kathleen.
Following magic / by Kathleen Duey ; illustrated by Sandara Tang. — 1st Aladdin hardcover ed.
p. cm. — (The faeries' promise)
ISBN 978-1-4169-8458-0 (hc)
Summary: Having escaped from the tower where she was trapped, the faerie Alida and her human helper Gavin try to elude capture by Lord Dunraven's men while they search for Alida's family.
[1. Fairies—Fiction. 2. Magic—Fiction.] I. Tang, Sandara, ill. II. Title.
PZ7.D8694Fo 2010
[Fic]—dc22
2009045801
ISBN 978-1-4169-8459-7 (pbk)
ISBN 978-1-4424-0980-4 (eBook)

Alida is a faerie princess. Gavin is a human boy. He helped her escape from Lord Dunraven's castle—and she saved his life. They are good friends. But old Lord Dunraven made a law sixty years ago that forbids people to have any contact with magical creatures. He didn't want the people in his lands to dream, to laugh aloud at faeries' tricks, or to be amazed at dragons flying overhead. He just wanted them to work hard. But a few people still tell stories about magic. It is very hard to make a story disappear. . . .

Chapter

1

The sun was rising.

It would be a warm, fine day.

Alida turned back to wave good-bye to Ruth Oakes and Gavin's grandmother.

They smiled at her, but Alida could tell they were worried. She was scared. She didn't want to leave Ruth's wonderful house near the town of Ash Grove. But she had no choice.

She glanced at Gavin.

He looked a little nervous too.

Alida was so grateful that he was coming with her.

They both stopped at the edge of the woods and both waved one last time.

Then they walked into the trees.

The grayish light of dawn was even dimmer beneath the old oaks. The trees smelled like home to Alida. That made her so happy—and so sad—that she stopped and closed her eyes, breathing deeply.

When she opened them, Gavin was looking at her. "Do you know which way we should go?"

Alida shook her head. Gavin had thought Ruth might know where the faeries had gone when old Lord Dunraven made his law, but she didn't. No one did.

"We just have to find the meadow I remember," Alida said. "I'm hoping my mother left something there for me."

Gavin lifted his eyebrows, but he didn't ask questions, and she was glad. She wasn't at all sure they would find anything in the meadow, and she had no idea what she would do if they didn't.

"Will you recognize the right place?" Gavin asked.

"Yes," Alida said. She was sure of that, even though she hadn't seen it in a long, long time. She remembered her family's home very clearly.

There was a noisy stream that ran across one end of the meadow.

At the other end there was a huge egg-shaped rock.

And there were many old oak trees, perfect for faerie nests. Everyone had slept in the treetops. She and her older sister had snuggled together if the night was chilly. Terra had always been patient with her, holding her hand when there was no moon and she was afraid of the dark. Terra was the elder, so when their mother got old, she would become queen. Alida knew Terra would be kind and fair, like their mother.

Alida sighed. She missed her family so much. "I hope it isn't too far from Ash Grove," she said, and turned to look at Gavin.

He shrugged. "We'll just keep searching until we find it."

Alida smiled at him.

They had both brought rolled-up blankets to keep them warm at night.

Her's was magical—her mother had woven it before she was born.

Gavin's was warm and soft, a gift from his grandmother. He had a flint and striker in his pocket in case they needed to make fire. He was carrying a cloth sack full of bread and cheese too.

Alida didn't have to bring anything to eat; she would be able to find proper faerie food—there were spring flowers everywhere.

Walking through the oak trees, Alida felt wonderful. The air was perfumed with dew and sunshine and spring. The forest was as beautiful as she remembered.

She was so excited.

She couldn't wait to find the meadow.

All of the faerie families had lived there when she was little.

All their children had played games and were taught magic. Alida had just begun to learn when Lord Dunraven took her away.

Alida sighed, remembering the faerie lights,

the stars, and how the stream had chuckled and whispered. Oh, how she had missed that sound. She had taught herself lifting magic and had learned to fly. She knew her family would be proud of her.

But of course they wouldn't be living in the meadow she remembered anymore.

Old Lord Dunraven's law had changed everything.

Alida walked a little faster, staying ahead of Gavin.

She didn't want him to see how sad it made her to think about her old home being empty. Once she had blinked away the tears, she glanced back at him.

"I wish Ruth Oakes and your grandmother had known where my family ended up."

"I think it was probably part of the faeries' promise not to tell humans where they were going," Gavin said.

Alida slowed until they were walking side by side. "Did your grandmother tell you that? Was it in the old stories?"

Gavin shook his head. "But it makes sense. If Lord Dunraven wanted to keep people and faeries from

being friends, he wouldn't want them living close."

"And to make the faeries keep their promise, he took me away," Alida said quietly.

Gavin nodded. "It must have been a terrible decision for your family."

Alida felt a stirring in her heart.

Locked in the tower in Lord Dunraven's castle, she had often wondered why her parents never came to help her. Now she knew why. They had been forced to make a promise to old Lord Dunraven.

Alida glanced up at the trees.

Her mother had known that Lord Dunraven would not hurt her as long as the faeries kept their promise to stay away from humans.

And he hadn't.

No one had said a single harsh word to her.

But she had been locked in a stone tower for a very long time.

She had been so lonely.

"Don't worry," Gavin said.

She glanced at him. "Do I look worried?"

He nodded. "But John will keep your secret and no one else knows you're not still locked in the tower. Lord Dunraven won't have any reason to suspect you are gone."

Alida hoped he was right.

But she still had to be careful.

She could never be sure when they might come upon a human being.

And if anyone realized she was a faerie, not just a small girl, people would talk.

The news would spread.

And then Lord Dunraven's guards *would* come looking for her. And if they found her—

"Alida?"

She turned; Gavin was pointing at a narrow road that ran between the trees. Without saying a word, they both veered away from it.

And as they walked, Alida pulled her shawl higher, making sure it covered her wings.

Chapter
2

Alida and Gavin walked until sunset that first day, then spread their blankets on the ground and slept, hidden in a stand of elm trees.

When they woke, Alida led the way again. "I can't remember where the meadow is," she admitted.

"Did your parents ever take you with them to Ash Grove?" Gavin asked.

She nodded. "A few times to Market Square. Everyone walked until the youngest ones were tired, then they flew and carried us."

He smiled. "What did they buy?"

"Honey candy," Alida said, remembering what

she had liked best. Then she thought about it. "Shoes sometimes," she said. "There was one cobbler who made them small enough for us. My mother liked him. He sold shoes for a fair price—and sometimes he would trade with us for some small magic."

Gavin looked surprised. "Faeries sound so much like people."

Alida nodded. "We are, I think. Except for the magic."

And the instant she said it, she realized how silly it sounded.

But Gavin just smiled, and she was almost sure he had understood. Magic was an important part of every faerie's life. But so were family and food and fun and everyday worries, just like humans.

The forest seemed endless. With every step Alida tried to recognize a tree, a hill, a stream, anything, but she couldn't.

By the second day it scared her a little.

Gavin kept telling her not to worry.

"But when we went to Market Square, I think it took only a day or two, even if we walked most of the way.

"Then tomorrow or the next day, if we don't find the meadow, we should change direction," Gavin said.

Alida nodded. It made sense.

The next day was sunny.

They crossed lots of meadows, but not the right one.

So the day after that they decided to travel west until noon, then turn northeast to follow a different route back toward Ash Grove.

Alida hoped every meadow they came to would be the one she remembered.

But none of them was.

Gavin began whistling as they walked, a merry tune. She knew he was trying to cheer her up.

He had changed since they left Lord Dunraven's cold stone castle. He stood straighter. He smiled more.

She knew she had changed too.

Locked inside the little room in Lord Dunraven's tower, she had gotten weak from eating human food. She had been so lonely, so sad.

But once Gavin began talking to her, bringing her flowers to eat and dew to drink, she had gotten stronger and stronger.

She stretched her wings beneath her shawl, wishing she could fly to search for the meadow.

It was amazing to feel the air rush past, to look down at the treetops.

And flying was much faster than walking!

But she couldn't risk being seen.

They avoided two little towns and a few farms. Then at midday, with the sun high overhead, Gavin spotted a deep, swift creek. They followed it for a while.

Alida gathered flowers.

When she had enough, they found a grassy place to sit. Gavin took brown bread and a piece of cheese out of his food sack. They ate without talking.

He kept glancing at her, then the horizon, then the forest behind them. She didn't ask him what he was thinking about. She didn't have to. He was thinking what she was.

Even though they both were sure that John would pretend Alida was still locked in the tower, Lord Dunraven might find out.

So his guards could gallop up at any moment.

They probably wouldn't.

But they might.

Alida looked into the forest. The trees were tall and beautiful, just as she remembered them. But there were many more human villages now. And there were paths everywhere.

She was still a faerie child; fairies had long, long lives. But a lot had changed during the sixty years she had been in Lord Dunraven's tower.

Was there a human town built in the meadow she remembered?

Alida ate her last two flowers, hoping Gavin

wouldn't see how much that thought upset her.

Once she finished, she washed her hands and face in the icy creek, then waited for Gavin to wash up. "It's cold," he said, picking up his food sack and his blanket. "But at least it's shallow here. Let's cross. I'll go first."

"Wait," Alida said. "There's no reason for either one of us to get soaked."

He glanced at her, then turned to peer into the trees. "You shouldn't," he whispered.

Alida nodded. "I know. But no one is nearby. And it's good for me to practice the lifting magic."

She waited for him to nod. Then she closed her eyes and concentrated.

It was a little easier each time.

When she opened her eyes, she smiled at Gavin. Then, very gently, she pushed the magic toward him and lifted him off the ground.

She held him carefully in the air, moving him slowly until he was on the other side of the stream.

Then she withdrew the magic, setting him down.

Once she had her shawl off, it took less than a heartbeat for her to fly across the creek. She landed and slid her shawl back over her wings.

Gavin was looking around, listening, making sure no one was close by.

Alida suddenly wondered how old he was. Ten? Eleven? He was already taller than she would ever be.

He had learned a lot more about being human than she had learned about being a faerie, too.

Alida was glad; most faeries lived to be a few hundred years old. She would have time to learn more about magic . . . about everything.

But she would have to work *very* hard to catch up with her sister and the other faerie children.

"Ready?" Gavin asked, pulling his food sack out of his blanket again so he wouldn't mash the bread as they walked.

She nodded, and he started off.

Alida followed, noticing that his food sack looked almost empty.

She had to remember that Gavin couldn't live on flowers and dew.

If they didn't find the meadow soon, she would try to talk him into going back to Ash Grove. She could keep searching by herself.

She didn't want him to leave.

She trusted Gavin completely. He was a good friend.

But this wasn't fair to him.

"Doesn't anything look familiar?" he asked over his shoulder.

Alida ran a few steps to catch up. "Not yet."

He sighed. "Maybe we should just try to find out where your family is living now. Ruth said there are fewer towns to the west and—"

"No, I have to find the meadow where we lived," Alida interrupted. "My mother might have left something to guide me."

Gavin blinked. "Something magical?"

Alida nodded. "And if she did, you should go home. Then your grandmother and Ruth won't have to worry about you anymore."

"They both understand," Gavin said. "You saved my life."

"And you saved mine," Alida said. A rustling sound from the trees behind them startled her.

Gavin turned. Alida peered into the shadows. They were both silent a long time, waiting, listening. The sound didn't come again.

"A fox?" Alida whispered.

Gavin nodded. "Or a squirrel looking for its supper?"

They began to walk. But Alida kept glancing back.

For the rest of the day she was a little uneasy.

She found lilies growing beside a stream. So her dinner was wonderful. Gavin's was not. He was almost out of food.

After they finished eating, they sat close together, their shoulders touching.

They watched the moon rise.

"I always wanted a little sister," he said quietly.

"I am much older than you are," she reminded him.

"And much smaller," he reminded her.

She nudged him.

He nudged her back.

And then they just stared at the stars.

Chapter

3

The next morning Alida heard another sound in the woods.

She spun around, tense and ready to run. This time it was a raccoon.

It bustled out of a plum thicket. When it saw them, it stopped, then changed direction.

Alida smiled at Gavin, feeling a little silly, but her heart was beating hard. "I am scared of Lord Dunraven's guards."

He nodded. "I am too. But they won't find you are gone."

"A few of them know you escaped," she reminded him.

He shrugged. "But they will never figure out how. Magic will never even cross their minds. They'll think they forgot to lock the door, that it was their fault. They'll never tell anyone."

Alida knew that made sense. Still, she kept listening, watching.

She really was scared.

Her room in Lord Dunraven's tower had been very small.

She had lived through sixty years of silence there.

If Gavin hadn't whispered through the bolted door, if they hadn't trusted each other, she would still be there. Alone.

"I always wanted an older brother," she said quietly.

He turned and shook his head. "No you didn't."

She smiled. "But I do now."

That night they found a sheltered place in a plum thicket.

They walked back and forth, gathering dried

grass to pile beneath their blankets. "It still feels odd to sleep on the ground," Gavin said.

Alida nodded. She knew he missed his bed.

It was odd for her, too, for a different reason. In the castle she'd had a human bed, and that had never been comfortable for her. But neither was this. Faeries made woven nests high in the trees.

"I love being back in the forest," she said quietly.

"I can't imagine being locked away like you were," Gavin said. "You were very brave. You still are."

Alida smiled, but she didn't feel brave.

She felt scared.

A breeze touched the trees, and the whispery sound made her pull her shawl close.

She fell asleep listening to crickets chirping and wood's mice running through the leaves.

In the morning she gathered flowers to eat while Gavin sat chewing the last of his bread and cheese.

"My grandmother gave me a few coins," he told

her. "Can you stay here while I find a village or a farmhouse—somewhere to buy bread?"

Alida looked at him. "I could fly high enough to spot the nearest village and—"

"But someone might see you," Gavin interrupted. He yawned and stretched. "We've been avoiding the paths. Next time we spot one, we can follow it until we spot the town. Then you can wait for me somewhere safe."

Alida nodded, wishing she could just go with him. "I don't like hiding," she said. "When I was little, there weren't many humans in the woods. But when we saw them, we were polite. My mother had human friends."

"I know," he said. "But it's against the law now."

Alida sighed. Old Lord Dunraven's law was terrible. And his gray-haired great-grandson was still making sure everyone obeyed it. "Maybe the next Lord Dunraven will be kinder," she said.

Gavin shook his head. "Probably not. This one

has no heir so it'll be one of his nephews. People say they are all selfish and spoiled." Hearing that made Alida sad. She started walking. She stared at the boulders and the streams.

Nothing looked familiar to her.

She found clover blossoms for breakfast.

Gavin chewed a few of them.

He was polite and said they tasted good, but Alida knew he was still very hungry.

They finally found a well-worn path. Alida flew up into a tree and hid while Gavin went on.

While he was gone, she had time to think.

What if it took until next winter for her to find her family's meadow? She wouldn't be terribly cold—faeries didn't mind snow and ice as much as people did—but Gavin would.

And even once she found the meadow, it could take a long time to discover what her mother had left for her.

If her mother had left *anything*. Maybe she had

been too afraid of old Lord Dunraven to leave anything magical behind.

Alida had no idea what she was going to do if that was true.

Where would she even start looking for her family?

She was glad to put her worries aside when she heard Gavin whistling. They walked back into the woods and found a place for him to eat the warm bread he had bought from a farmer's wife.

"You don't have to do this," she said.

"Do what?"

"You don't have to help me any more than you already have."

Gavin stopped chewing. He looked puzzled. "I know that."

"I mean, you could just go back to Ash Grove today."

"Would you rather travel alone?"

"No!" she said. "But who knows how long this will take?" She gestured at the endless trees.

He was silent. Then he shrugged. "I want to make sure you find your family."

"Thank you," she said, becasue it was too complicated to explain that even though she wanted him to stay, she felt terrible about it.

And in an odd way, it felt wrong to ask a human to help search for something magical. But he was the only one she could possibly trust with something this important.

Late that afternoon they walked up a long hill.

Gavin was a little ways ahead by the time the land flattened out. He stopped and turned back, waving. "Come see this!"

She ran to catch up, and once she was close, he pointed.

The sun was shining through the branches of an enormous old oak tree. It made the leaves look like copper and gold. "Every meadow seems magical enough for faeries," he said.

Alida smiled at him.

Suddenly, he gripped her arm. "Did you hear that?"

Alida caught her breath and listened. It sounded like hoofbeats. It was . . .

Too heavy for deer.

Horses? She stared in the direction of the sound. Dunraven's guards?

"Follow me!" Gavin whispered, and ran toward the nearest stand of trees.

Alida ran for ten or twelve paces, pulling off her shawl. Then she leapt into the air, flying straight up so that she could see.

Gavin kept running.

Moments later Alida swooped low, landing beside him.

He slowed a little so that she could keep up.

"It's not Lord Dunraven's guards," she told him. "The horses don't have armor."

Once they were safe in a thick stand of ash trees, both of them still breathing hard, Gavin frowned at her.

She knew why.

She had been foolish to fly like that. What if it had been guards? What if one of them had seen her?

Alida and Gavin stood side by side, hidden in a tangle of branches, watching as the riders came nearer—there were two men and a boy who looked about Gavin's age.

Their horses were beautiful.

All three were deep gray with white manes and tails. The riders wore bright clothing. They had capes that billowed out behind them.

Alida peered out as they galloped past. "Who are they?" she whispered.

"Nobles," Gavin said once they were gone.

"Lord Dunraven's relatives?" Alida asked.

Gavin shrugged. "Maybe. There are lords in all the lands."

Alida blinked. "How many are there?"

"I don't know," Gavin said. "There's Lord

28

Ermaedith. And Lord Kaybale. And . . ." He paused, then shook his head. "There are four or five besides Dunraven, I think. A lot of them are related. They all hate magic."

"All of them?"

"That's what people say." Gavin kicked at a stone, then looked at her. "You can't just fly like that. If anyone sees you, Lord Dunraven *will* hear about it eventually. Please, Alida. You have to be careful."

"I will," she said and she meant it. But the truth was, she hadn't thought about whether or not she should fly—not for an instant.

She had just done it.

When she was scared, flying came as naturally to her as running did to Gavin.

Chapter
4

Alida and Gavin passed through twenty or more of lovely meadows over the next two days.

Every evening they made a little camp.

Every morning they made sure they erased every single sign that they had been there.

Some of the meadows they saw had streams running through them.

A few had big stones that jutted up out of the ground.

None had the huge egg-shaped boulder Alida remembered so well.

Her sister had boosted her up the side of the rock

over and over so that she could climb to the top, spread her wings wide, then jump off and glide to the ground.

That was how very young faeries strengthened their wings.

That was how they learned to fly.

One morning, Alida and Gavin had to cross a river. She lifted him then flew across as she had before. That afternoon, clouds rolled in and hid the sun.

"Maybe we should look for a village," Gavin said. "I could get more food, and we could find a place to wait out the storm."

Alida nodded.

As they walked, the air got cooler and the clouds darkened.

They kept watching for paths to follow. But before they could find one, they heard someone shouting.

The voice was high, angry, but they were too far away to understand a single word.

Alida glanced at Gavin. "Maybe we should see if she needs help?"

He nodded. "But you have to stay hidden, Alida."

"I will," she promised.

As they got closer, the shouting became weeping. Alida could see that the trees thinned up ahead.

"Wait here," Gavin whispered. "I'll come back as quick as I can."

Alida stopped. "I'll find a place to watch, in case you need help."

"Just stay hidden," he said as he set down his blanket and the cloth sack.

Then he disappeared, walking past the last of the trees and into the clearing.

Alida tied her shawl tighter around her shoulders.

She found a place where she could see through the branches without anyone being able to spot her.

It was a human girl.

She was sitting on the ground, hunched over.

Alida watched Gavin walk toward her.

He stopped halfway and glanced back. Alida knew he was making sure that she was well hidden. Then he went on.

Alida could tell the exact instant that Gavin spoke, because the girl jumped to her feet, startled.

Alida tried to hear what Gavin was saying, but she couldn't.

Then the girl began talking—much louder than Gavin had. Her face was red from crying, and she was furious. "I was just grazing our sheep," she said, "when some people rode up." She kicked at the dirt. "They galloped in circles around me, scaring the sheep until they ran off in every direction." She wiped at her tears. "I've never lost track of them before. We're weavers. Without the sheep's wool to make yarn, my family will starve."

Gavin asked her a question that Alida couldn't hear.

The girl shook her head. "They wore fancy capes and rode well-bred grays."

Alida was sure the girl was talking about the riders she and Gavin had seen.

She stepped farther back into the trees. Her family had never kept sheep—wool was too heavy for faerie clothing. But they had kept goats for milk and cheese in the winter, when there were no flowers to eat.

Alida remembered the goats getting scattered in storms sometimes, if the thunder was loud enough to scare them into running. She had helped Terra look for them.

They hadn't run very far. And they had stayed together.

Alida dropped her shawl on the ground, spread her wings, and leapt upward.

She was at the treetops in an instant. Hovering, she turned in a quick circle, then did it again, more slowly.

There.

She saw a patch of cream-white through the green of the trees.

She flew closer.

It was six sheep, their tails switching back and forth. They were nervous, wandering in thick brush.

Six? No. Alida spotted two more.

There were eight sheep.

Alida flew back and dropped to the ground, extending her wings just enough to land lightly.

She put on her shawl again and walked out of the trees. "I saw your sheep!" she called.

Gavin turned and stared at her.

The girl ran toward her. "Where?"

Alida pointed. "That way. Eight of them. Fairly close, and I . . . ," she began, then didn't finish because the girl was sprinting past her. She kept running and didn't look back.

"Alida!"

She turned.

Gavin looked angry. "You can't do that again," he said once he was close enough to speak in a low voice.

Alida felt herself getting upset. "If I hadn't, the

36

sheep might have wandered off. I heard what she told you . . . her family could have starved."

"But your wings make a whirring sound," he said. "I could hear them. It's not very loud, but still, that girl might have—"

"I know." Alida squared her shoulders. "I just wanted to help. She was so scared."

Gavin nodded. "People in Ash Grove are poor, but she made it sound like things are even worse here."

"Why would they scatter her sheep?" Alida asked. "Why would anyone do something like that?"

Gavin shrugged. "Lord Dunraven and his friends have galloped through Ash Grove a few times, racing their horses past Market Square and all the way across the river bridge. They could have hurt someone. I guess they don't care."

Alida was astonished. "Everyone in Ash Grove must have been angry."

He sighed. "The towns all belong to Lord Dunraven, just like the forests do."

"No one can own a forest," Alida said.

Gavin looked at her. "Lord Dunraven does. All the lords own the lands they rule. And the people who live there are bound in service to them."

"The faeries aren't!" she said, sure she was right, even though she had been very young when she was taken away from her family. "Faerie children are taught that everyone shares the forests, the sun, the moon, the wind. . . ."

Alida closed her hands into fists, too angry to go on.

Gavin didn't say anything for a long time.

Alida understood why. It had been like this his whole life.

But she was much older than he was, and she knew that things had once been very different. Humans had once had faerie, unicorn, and dragon friends. Maybe that had kept the lords of the lands from bullying them.

When Gavin did speak, he sounded sad. "I

think I know why old Dunraven made your family leave."

She nodded, understanding him instantly.

Faeries would have stopped that horse race through Ash Grove—with magic.

A low roll of thunder made them both look up at the sky.

Gavin turned in the direction the girl had gone. "We should make sure she doesn't need help."

Alida nodded and tied her shawl closer.

When they caught up, the girl was guiding ten sheep along a path. She was almost dancing, she was so happy.

"I found the other two!" she called when she saw them. "Please come with me and meet my family. My mother will be so grateful."

"Would your family have a little bread to sell us?" Alida asked.

"They will be happy to give you bread," the girl said.

Gavin thanked her. "That would be a great help. We have a long way to travel."

"My name is Holly," she said. Alida and Gavin introduced themselves.

They all walked together, staying behind the sheep. Alida kept glancing at the sky.

There was no lightning yet, and only a little thunder rumbling, but the clouds were thick.

Holly knew every barely-there path, and where to find the shortcuts between them.

So did the sheep.

Before long they were on a road wide enough for carts and wagons.

Alida walked carefully, making sure that her shawl stayed in place, her blanket tucked under one arm.

Gavin had been right about the people being poor.

The houses were all very small.

The people were wearing old clothes with patches sewn over the places where the cloth had worn thin.

"What's the name of this village?" Gavin asked.

Holly shooed the sheep along, then turned to answer. "Oak's End." She pointed to a rise in the distance. "After you get to that ridge, there aren't any more oak trees. It's all ash and alders and poplars."

Alida smiled. Knowing that made things easier. If there were no oak trees, it was time to change direction again. The wide meadow where she was born had a dozen huge oak trees in it.

Holly's house was small, but it was warm and very clean.

Her parents were as nice as she was.

They insisted that Gavin and Alida join them for supper.

Alida took only a little of the human food for herself and ate tiny bites.

Gavin ate like a wolf, savoring the roast chicken and buttered corn.

Alida watched him. She had eaten her fill of flowers every day, but it was clear that he hadn't been full for a long time. She was ashamed that she hadn't noticed.

"Thank you for helping our daughter," Holly's father said when they had finished.

Gavin nodded. "It was a simple thing—and we both thank you for this wonderful supper."

Alida nodded.

She watched Holly's parents smile and glance at each other.

Gavin was very good at talking to people.

He was good at being a friend, too.

He certainly would have noticed if she had been hungry half the time. He would have tried to find more food for her.

Alida realized something: She had lived alone in Lord Dunraven's tower most of her life. Magic wasn't the only thing she needed to learn.

"Do you know what your name means, Alida?" Holly's mother asked. "It's a very old one. Did you know that?"

Alida shook her head.

"It means 'small winged one,'" Holly's mother

told her. "It's probably an old faerie name. My great-grandmother was called Kendra, which means—"

Holly's father cleared his throat. He was frowning.

"I know we aren't supposed to talk about faeries," Holly's mother said. "But my grandmother told me all the old tales, and—"

Holly's father cleared his throat again. He was staring at his wife.

"I wonder if it's going to storm," she said.

No one answered.

She looked embarrassed. "I just meant that Alida is a lovely name for a lovely girl."

Alida ducked her head, embarrassed.

A rumble of thunder made them all look up.

"There's no room in the house," Holly's mother said. "But you are more than welcome to sleep in our barn loft tonight."

Gavin answered her and Alida listened carefully.

He didn't just say thank you, he thanked her for saving them a long, cold night in bad weather.

Alida hoped that her own clumsy thank you's to Gavin's grandmother and Ruth Oakes had been good enough. If she ever saw them again, she would try to explain how much their kindness had meant.

After supper, Holly asked her parents for food Alida and Gavin could carry with them.

Her mother came back from the kitchen with bread, cheese, and two apples from their root cellar.

Then Holly led them outside.

The sheep were sleepy, baaing just a little when she opened the heavy door.

The barn smelled like fresh hay and wool. The planked walls were thick, and no wind came through. They would be safe and warm.

Holly led the way up the ladder. It was a big loft, only half full of hay.

"I could walk with you for a ways tomorrow," she

said. Then she blushed. "I mean me and the sheep. I have to graze them every day."

"There might not be good grass the way we are going," Gavin told her.

Holly looked disappointed and Alida wondered if she got tired of being alone with the sheep all the time.

Probably.

But Alida knew Holly couldn't come with them. It would be too hard to explain what they were looking for—and why they had to hurry.

Alida hunched her shoulders, then pushed them back. Her wings hurt from having her shawl tied so tightly over them all day.

"Maybe we can come back one day," Gavin said. "Just to visit."

Holly smiled. "Oh, I hope so." Then she said good night and went back down the ladder.

Alida and Gavin heard the barn door open, then close.

"She seems very nice," Gavin said.

Alida nodded. "She does. And it's going to be like this forever, isn't it? For me, I mean. I will never be able to have another human friend."

"Maybe not," Gavin said sadly.

Then they both stopped talking.

They fluffed up piles of hay and folded their blankets in half lengthwise.

Alida slid into her makeshift bed and listened to the wind until she fell asleep.

Chapter

5

After midnight a big storm rolled in, rumbling, the wind rising.

Thunder woke Alida in the dark.

When it quieted, she could hear Gavin breathing slow and deep and knew he was asleep.

She closed her eyes, but the storm kept her awake. It scared her.

Over and over, flashes of lightning lit the barn for an instant, then blinked out.

The sheep were uneasy too.

Alida could hear them moving around, bleating quietly.

She made herself close her eyes, and eventually she went back to sleep.

Before dawn, a sharp, hissing whisper woke Alida.

Holly was pulling at her blanket, holding a little candle lantern, her eyes full of fear.

"Get up!" she was saying, over and over. Her voice was shaking.

Gavin stood up. "What's wrong?'

"There are guards in our house," Holly whispered. "They made my mother cook supper for them and then said they were going to sleep out here and—"

Alida scrambled to her feet and then remembered her shawl.

It was too late. Holly's eyes went wide. "You really are a faerie?"

Voices from the house startled them all.

"They're coming!" Holly said. "If they catch me out here—"

"We can go out the loft door," Gavin said, looking at Alida. "It faces the woods."

"No we can't!" Holly said. "It's too far to jump."

Gavin took her hand. "There's no time to explain, just get the door open."

Holly led them across the loft in the dark and found the latch.

When the planked door swung open, rain spattered in.

"Can you lower us both at once?" Gavin asked Alida.

She nodded. "I think so. Yes."

"Blow out your candle and close your eyes," he said to Holly.

She was breathing hard and looked scared, but she put out the lantern and shut her eyes. Gavin took her hand. "It's like a dream," he said. "Like you are floating. Don't make a sound."

She nodded.

Alida gathered the magic quickly.

She lifted them a little, just a little, then pushed them out the narrow door. She heard Holly gasp, and Gavin whispering as she lowered them to the ground.

Once they were safe, she flew out, hovered long enough to push the loft door closed, then glided downward.

Holly hugged her and whispered in her ear. "I will never tell anyone about you," she promised.

And then she was gone, running back toward the house, disappearing into the darkness.

It was still sprinkling and there was a little wind.

Alida and Gavin ran and kept running until they were a long way from Holly's house.

The forest smelled like rain and woods and sky.

"Do you think Lord Dunraven sent them?" Alida asked once they slowed down.

Gavin shrugged. "I hope not. I hope they just wanted to get out of the storm.

"You should never have let her see your wings," Gavin said after a long moment.

"I was barely awake," she defended herself.

He glanced at her. "I know, but you have to get used to hiding them."

Alida nodded.

"If Holly tells someone—" he began.

"She won't," Alida interrupted.

"You don't know that," Gavin said. "You saw how poor they are. What if someone offered her enough coins to feed her whole family all winter? We shouldn't have told them our names."

Alida didn't know what to say. But she knew he was right.

Holly would have to think of her own family first.

Gavin stopped. "Which way should we go?"

Alida pointed, and they started back toward Ash Grove again, veering so they would be following paths they hadn't used before. She was more afraid than she had ever been in her life. She wanted to find the meadow she remembered, and soon.

The rain spattered down again, not hard and not

for very long, but it was chilly, and they shuffled along, their heads down. Gavin was shivering.

"I wish the storm would stop," he said.

Alida knew she wasn't as cold as he was. "If we pass a farm, maybe we could hide in someone else's barn until it's over."

He nodded, rubbing his hands together. She put her blanket around his shoulders, then glanced up at the sky.

It was getting lighter. Dawn was coming. She could see a line of trees in the distance.

"Those look like old oaks," she said.

Gavin nodded, and they walked faster.

They came to a wide meadow and started across it just as the rain began again.

Alida wished she knew rain magic, but she didn't know any kind of weather magic yet. Grown-up faeries never got cold or wet, except in fierce storms.

"Are you cold?" Gavin asked. "Do you want your blanket back?"

She shook her head and was about to tell him how her mother could stop raindrops in midair.

But then lightning flashed.

It was so bright it hurt her eyes.

But for an instant she could see a familiar shape at the far end of the meadow.

She shouted at Gavin, then ran.

And when running wasn't fast enough, she pulled off her shawl and flew. In a few heartbeats, soaking wet and out of breath, Alida stood before the egg-shaped rock.

It was exactly the way she had remembered it.

One side was less steep. That was where Terra had boosted her up so she could practice gliding.

The stone was a lovely brown-red color, darkened by the rain.

She ran her hands over it.

She was crying when Gavin finally caught up.

"Is this it?" he asked her, smiling.

She nodded.

He danced a few steps, then kissed her forehead.

Alida was breathless and happy and scared all at once.

What if her mother hadn't left anything for her to find? It was possible. Maybe she had been afraid someone else might find it.

Alida pressed her cheek against the stone and closed her eyes, ignoring the sprinkling rain. Being here, seeing the meadow again, her memories were coming back.

She remembered so many things about this place.

She could picture the faerie nests in the trees, everyone calling good night across the darkness.

She remembered the sound of happy music in the air, the everyday joy of magic.

She closed her eyes and she could see her parents' faces. And Terra's.

And all her cousins and aunts and uncles.

For an instant Alida thought she heard her mother calling her name.

Her eyes flew open.

She spun in a circle.

But no one was near. There was only the sound of the light rain pattering the leaves of the oak trees.

Gavin was staring at her.

"I thought I heard my mother's voice," she told him. "It seemed so clear and so close."

"Could that mean the magic is nearby?" Gavin asked quietly.

Alida took a long breath. "Maybe." She looked up at the huge stone. If her mother had left something, it would be carefully hidden.

She peered into the woods. "I don't know where to start looking," she admitted. "Or what to look for."

"In my grandmother's stories there were magic stones and talking birds, and trees with golden leaves," Gavin said.

"There can be magic in anything," Alida told him. "Every faerie child is taught that."

Gavin nodded, then kept quiet as she walked all the way around the huge stone.

Alida couldn't see anything unusual. Nothing.

She walked around the stone a second time, and still couldn't see anything but spring grass, weeds, and small, ordinary, grayish stones.

Alida looked at Gavin. "Do *you* see anything that seems magical?"

Gavin's eyebrows arched and he turned in a circle. "No. But I don't know what to look for."

"I don't either," Alida said.

The rain fell a little harder, then lightened again. She squinted, looking at every part of the egg-shaped stone.

Nothing caught her eye.

She looked at the trees across the clearing. The sky was brightening behind the layer of clouds, and she recognized the oak she had slept in when she was little. It had one long, low branch she remembered sitting on to watch Terra practice flying.

Her eyes stung. To keep Gavin from seeing how close she was to crying, she stared at the ground.

It was covered with green spring grass. There were dandelions, too. Alida picked one and ate it.

Dandelions weren't sweet like roses and lilies.

They had a sharp, lively taste.

She reached down to pick a few more, suddenly remembering that her mother loved them—that she liked them better than sweeter flowers.

The memory was precious.

For a moment Alida had to hold back tears again.

Then she noticed something.

There were bright yellow dandelion flowers.

There were also empty stems.

The storm wind had scattered all their seeds. That was how dandelions planted themselves. The wind sailed the fluff-topped seeds over the whole meadow and into the woods.

But there was one stem that still held its fluffy umbrella of seeds.

Alida bent over it, puzzled.

She glanced up at Gavin, then back at the dandelion.

"What?" he asked her.

She pointed. "Its seeds are all still there. Even after all the wind and rain."

"Could it be magical?" he asked.

Alida smiled. "Maybe. When I was little we used to blow the seeds into the air to watch them fly." She picked the dandelion.

She held it carefully and pulled off a single seed.

It was perfect, and soaked with rainwater.

She held it high between two fingers and turned her face upward.

A few raindrops hit her face as she puckered her lips.

Feeling silly, her cheeks wet, she blew at the dandelion seed, opening her fingers to let it drop.

But the seed rose upward! Then it stopped and hung in midair.

When a gust of wind came across the meadow, the dandelion seed bobbed a little, but that was all.

It wasn't shoved forward; it didn't spiral to the ground.

Alida glanced at Gavin.

He looked amazed.

It had to be magic.

The dandelion seed was floating in the air, not moving where the wind should have taken it. The rain suddenly came down harder, and the seed just stayed where it was, moving gently up and down.

"What are we supposed to do?" Gavin asked her.

"Maybe it will lead us to my family," she said slowly, afraid she might be wrong, but hoping with all her heart.

Gavin hitched her blanket high on his shoulders and shook his head. "A dandelion seed?"

She nodded. "I think so."

"I wasn't sure what to expect," Gavin admitted. "But it wasn't this."

Alida smiled.

It seemed a little silly, even to her.

But her mother was very clever.

Someone might have picked up a brightly-colored stone. Anyone could have spotted a lavender rose or a tree with a golden leaf.

Alida stared at the dandelion seed, then glanced at Gavin. He was watching her.

She put the dried dandelion bloom inside the folds of her shawl and tied the ends carefully to hold it there.

Then she looked up at the seed again. "Which way should we go?" she asked it.

For a long moment the dandelion hung in midair.

Then it slid to one side and swooped back.

It twirled in a circle. Then it rose upward.

"What's it doing?" Gavin whispered.

Alida had no idea, but he was looking at her, so she took a guess. "Maybe," she said quietly, "it's waking up? It's been waiting for me for a long time."

Gavin laughed aloud and she smiled at him.

"It's wonderful somehow," he said, "to see something that make no sense at all."

Alida nodded. It was. Even though she was a faerie, even though she had taught herself to fly, it had been a very long time since she had seen this kind of magic.

Chapter

6

The seed began to move slowly forward.

"Should we follow it?" Gavin whispered.

Alida nodded.

They started walking.

Gavin glanced at her. "It's moving in the opposite direction of the wind, now."

Alida smiled.

The dandelion seed led them across the wide meadow. Then, instead of going straight on, it turned.

Alida was looking upward, watching the dandelion, not Gavin, and she stumbled into him. He caught her hand so that she didn't fall.

A few minutes later it happened again, but it was Gavin who stumbled.

"I wish it would go a little slower," she said clearly, "and fly a little lower."

And the instant she said it, the seed drifted back and forth, slowing, floating downward. It stopped at eye level and waited for them to catch up.

Once they were close, it started off again.

Slower.

Lower.

"Was that magic?" Gavin whispered. "Did it just grant your wish?"

Alida nodded, feeling strange and wonderful. "I think so. My mother can do all sorts of things with simple wishes."

"If all your wishes will come true," Gavin said, "maybe you should wish for the sun to come out."

Alida looked at him. His cheeks were pink with cold. She shook her head, knowing that was exactly the kind of thing she shouldn't wish for. It was one of the first things her mother had taught her.

"Small wishes are the kindest," she said.

Gavin looked at her. "Why?"

"It's the first thing faeries teach their children," she said. "Small wishes are best because they cause the fewest problems."

Gavin jumped over a fallen log, then walked beside her again. "Getting rid of a cold spring rain seems like a small wish," he said.

Alida glanced at him. "But what if the farms and the flowers need rain?"

Gavin pulled her blanket close around his neck. "Oh. We would be warmer, but people and faeries might not have as much food stored for next winter."

Alida nodded.

Gavin blew into his cupped hands to warm them.

"I wonder if any humans have ever learned to work magic."

Alida shrugged. "I don't know."

"Could they learn it?" he asked.

Alida didn't answer him because she had no idea if humans could learn magic or not. But she was pretty sure that faeries would never teach them. "My father said humans weren't careful enough to use magic."

Gavin smiled. "Someone like Ruth Oakes would be. Or my grandmother."

Alida knew he was right.

As they walked, she thought about it, and couldn't remember any of the faeries ever teaching magic to humans.

Alida glanced at Gavin. He was staring at the floating dandelion seed. And he was still smiling.

"It's changing direction a little," he said, pointing.

Alida nodded.

With its puffy white cap still soaked with rain, the seed was drifting eastward. It was turning almost straight into the wind.

They followed it into a stand of trees.

"It's probably impossible now," Gavin said sadly, breaking the silence.

Alida looked at him. "What is?"

"No faerie would dare to teach a human magic," he said. "Because of Dunraven's law."

"I'm sorry," she said quietly.

Gavin looked at her. "It isn't your fault. And maybe it's impossible for people to learn magic anyway. I've never heard of it."

He reached out and touched her cheek. "You're cold. Here," he said, and started to give her back her blanket.

She shook her head. "Keep it."

He started to argue with her, but she walked faster to warm them both up. The dandelion moved faster too, staying ahead of them.

As they came out of the trees, she looked up at the sky. The clouds were light gray now. The wind was calming too.

The dandelion seed kept floating through the wind.

They followed it up hills and across creeks and

through thick stands of oak and pine trees.

"We've walked a long way today," Gavin said as they started up another steep hill.

"We have," Alida agreed. She could tell he was tired. So was she.

But they didn't stop or even slow down. They kept going.

"We can't follow the magic in the dark, can we?" Gavin asked when the sun was low in the sky.

"I don't know," Alida admitted.

"Are you tired?"

She sighed and nodded. "But I'm not sure the magic knows we need to sleep."

"We have to find out," Gavin said

He caught her hand and they stopped, watching the dandelion seed.

It slowed, swung back and forth for a moment, then drifted up onto a wide tree branch and settled there.

Alida walked closer to look at it. She blew at it

gently. It rocked back and forth like a plain dandelion seed would have, but it stayed on the branch.

She blew harder and the same thing happened.

The magic was holding it in place.

"I think it knows we need to rest," she said, turning to look at Gavin.

At first they sat side by side on a fallen log, too tired to do anything else.

The rain was over, Alida was almost sure. The clouds were thinning. She could see a few stars.

"We need to make a fire to dry our clothes and blankets," Gavin said.

Alida found a tangle of slender twigs. It was an old crow's nest that the wind had blown out of a tree.

Gavin spotted a dead branch, and they broke it into pieces.

After a long search they dug into a deep mound of wet leaves and found dry ones underneath. Once they had everything ready, Gavin took out his flint and striker.

The leaves crackled. The wood began to burn.

The warmth felt wonderful. They both stood as close to the flames as they could. Their damp clothing steamed and began to dry.

They draped their blankets over tree limbs above the fire so that they would dry out too.

When Gavin opened his food sack, he offered Alida some of the little bit of bread and cheese that he had left. She shook her head. "An apple?" he said.

"I've never eaten one," she told him.

He smiled. "I think you'll like it."

Alida took the fruit from him, and he watched as she sniffed it.

It smelled like flowers.

She took a little bite and was surprised at how sweet it was.

"I don't know if other faeries eat apples," she told him. "But I like them very much."

Gavin looked pleased.

Then he ate his own supper.

They didn't talk very much. They were too tired.

Gavin found more firewood and dragged over a much bigger log to sit on.

Alida discovered a deep crack between two big rocks—a safe place to put the dandelion for the night.

When their clothes and their blankets were dry, they wrapped themselves up and sat close together watching the fire.

The rain storm was gone, but the ground was still too wet to lie on. So they leaned against each other and went to sleep sitting up.

Chapter

7

Alida woke first.

The sun was just coming up and the sky was blue.

The fire had burned down to white ashes.

She squinted to see the seed on the limb above their heads, but it wasn't quite light enough. She moved a little, trying to spot it. Gavin awakened.

"Is it there?" he asked quietly.

"If it isn't, I think we could use one of the other seeds," she said, standing on her tiptoes, hoping it was true.

Gavin stretched and yawned, then stood up. He was taller. "It's there," he said.

Alida smiled, relieved.

They rolled up their blankets.

Alida tucked the dandelion into her shawl, then tied the ends tightly.

They mounded up handfuls of damp dirt, burying the ashes from the fire.

When they were sure it was out, Gavin stood back. "We should be even more careful than we have been."

Alida understood what he meant. It would be incredibly foolish to leave a trail that anyone could follow, especially now. They had to be getting close.

Together, they checked the bushes for frayed threads from their clothes or their blankets.

They used branches to scuff away their footprints and scattered leaves over the ground.

Once they were finished, they stood side by side, looking up at the dandelion seed. It was lying motionless sideways on the tree bark.

"Should we just start walking?" Gavin whispered.

Alida looked at him. "I don't know."

She took one step.

The dandelion seed swayed a little.

She took another step.

It rose into the air.

She began to walk, slowly.

It sailed against the breeze, caught up, passed her, then led the way.

"Amazing," Gavin whispered.

Alida smiled. Magic was so lovely, so full of joy. Oh, how she had missed it.

The dandelion seed led them into woods so thick that sunlight could not reach the ground.

Then they crossed a wide meadow.

At first Alida gathered wildflowers and ate them as she walked.

But the meadow was so big that she glanced back a few times to make sure no one was following them.

She noticed Gavin doing the same thing.

"The rain helped hide us," she said.

He nodded. "Not even Dunraven's guards would

ride in weather like that if they could avoid it."

"But now?" Alida said, looking up at the bright sky, then back at Gavin.

She looked at the little white puff that was bobbing up and down in the air ahead of them, waiting. "We should walk in the woods so that no one sees us," she said slowly and clearly.

The instant she said it, the little seed slid through the air sideways, toward the edge of the forest.

And for the rest of the day they stayed out of meadows, both small and wide.

That night was dry and still. They slept until the sun rose.

Alida ate a few of the flowers she had gathered the day before.

Gavin ate a bite of bread and a bite of cheese.

Alida knew why. He was nearly out of food. She shouldn't have eaten his apple. "Maybe we will see a farm today."

He shook his head. "I don't think your mother's magic will guide us anywhere near a farm or a town."

Alida sighed. Of course he was right.

"I think my family will have at least some foods you like," Alida said. "They keep goats and make cheese for winter food."

Gavin nodded. "I'll manage. And I won't be staying very long."

Alida turned her head so he couldn't see how much that upset her.

They spent that night deep in the forest again.

The next day at dawn Alida woke with a start.

The sound was faint, but she knew exactly what it was.

Faerie flutes!

She woke Gavin.

"Shh!" she said before he could say a single word. "Listen! Can you hear that?"

His forehead crinkled. He closed his eyes. Then he shook his head. "Hear what?"

"Faerie music," Alida said. She rolled her blanket and put the dandelion in a safe place inside her shawl. Then she erased their footprints while Gavin looked for threads. It was hard for her not to fidget while he rolled up his own blanket.

Alida led the way, walking faster and faster, wishing she could fly.

The dandelion matched its speed to hers.

So did Gavin.

When they finally came out of the trees and saw the beautiful meadow, they stopped.

Alida stared, her heart rising. Her family's new home was exactly what she had hoped it would be.

It was a beautiful and very busy faerie meadow.

The flute players were sitting in a circle.

Faeries were flying in every direction, doing all kinds of work, singing and talking.

There was a rock outcropping on the far side of the wide clearing.

Alida could see faerie children learning to glide.

"Are those faerie nests?" Gavin asked quietly. He pointed.

Alida looked up. She could see the usual woven limbs and the bright colors of faerie blankets. "Yes!"

Gavin tugged gently at her shawl. "You can take this off now."

Alida smiled. She untied the ends and held the dandelion in her hand while Gavin lifted the shawl off her shoulders and draped it over his arm.

They stood side by side until she took a long breath and looked up at him.

"Are you ready?" he asked.

"I think so," she said.

And they walked forward together.

Chapter

8

Alida felt strange. She was happier than she could ever remember being.

But she was nervous, too. She was a stranger here.

She hadn't seen her family in a very, *very* long time. She hadn't seen any faeries at all since she was little.

As she and Gavin walked down the slope into the meadow, the faerie children stopped their games and whispered to one another.

One flew high into a tree, and three baby faeries suddenly peered down from their nest.

But they were not staring at her, Alida realized.

They were looking at Gavin. Because of Lord Dunraven's law, most of the young faeries had never seen a human before.

The musicians suddenly stopped playing.

Alida could see how startled they were. Everyone was. The whispers got louder and louder.

"Maybe I should have waited in the trees," Gavin said quietly.

"Alida? Alida!"

The shout from above startled them both.

Alida looked up and saw her father flying toward her.

Smiling, so excited she could barely stand still, she watched him angle downward.

He flew lower and lower, until his feet touched the ground.

He ran the last few steps, kissed her forehead, and took the dandelion bloom out of her hand. He blew on it and it disappeared.

Alida could not speak.

Her father picked her up, careful of her wings, and swung her in a circle.

"I am so glad to see you," he said over and over. "Welcome home!"

When he finally set her down, he turned and shouted. "Someone tell the queen! Tell her Alida is home!"

Two faeries leapt into the air and flew off. The others stood still, staring.

Alida's father touched her cheek, then he glanced at Gavin.

"He helped me escape," Alida said. "Lord Dunraven—"

"We can talk about all that later," her father interrupted her gently. "You're home, and that's all that matters to me now."

Alida leaned on him and watched the faeries fly across the meadow. They disappeared into the woods on the far side.

A moment later a faerie girl came running out of

the trees. She jumped into the air and flew fast.

"Terra?" Alida breathed. She fluttered her own wings and rose up to meet her sister.

Terra was even more beautiful than Alida remembered. And she flew with the grace of a willow tree in the wind.

They hovered, smiling at each other, neither of them knowing what to say at first.

"Are you all right?" Terra whispered. "It must have been terrible."

Alida nodded, blinking back tears. "I am so happy to see you." She looked down at Gavin. Faeries were coming toward them from every direction.

She saw some familiar faces—aunts and uncles and cousins that she barely remembered. The younger ones hadn't been born when old Lord Dunraven made his law.

The faeires were all smiling up at her—and glancing at Gavin. They looked worried.

She took Terra's hand and they landed side by

side on the grass. Alida took a deep breath. She was about to shout that without Gavin, she would still be a captive. But her father shook his head and pointed.

"Your mother is coming. She will know what to say."

Alida watched her mother fly closer and closer. Her hair was shining in the sun, and her eyes were full of love.

Alida began to cry. All the years of being afraid and alone were over. She really was home.

Her mother held her close and whispered in her ear. "I was so afraid I would never see you again, daughter. Welcome home."

"A feast!" someone shouted. "Our princess returns! What better reason for a feast!"

There was laughter. It turned into cheering.

Alida stepped back from her mother.

She couldn't see Gavin. Then she spotted him walking away beside her father.

She felt her mother's hand on her arm. "Your

father will take good care of the human boy. You must come with me."

"Gavin saved me," Alida said. "If he hadn't helped me escape, I would still be locked in Dunraven's tower."

Sadness crossed her mother's face. "I was hoping one of the Dunravens had gotten rid of that terrible law." She sighed. "There will be hard times ahead for all of us. The humans will do what Dunraven tells them to do."

"And the faeries will obey you," Alida said.

Her mother laughed. "Terra won't. She wants nothing to do with being the next queen and refuses to learn anything. But she has become one of our best musicians."

Alida blinked, unsure what to say. Terra had to be the next queen; she was the elder daughter.

Alida's mother leaned close to her ear. "I am so very glad you found a way to come home. And now we need to plan a feast."

She straightened up and pitched her voice higher

and much, much louder. "Let's prepare a wonderful homecoming for our Alida!"

The whole meadow quieted for a few heartbeats.

Then the faeries began talking again, all at once.

Alida's mother bent close. "They will stop talking and get busy in a moment. For your human boy we have cheese and honey. But I won't be able to get yeast or wheat to make bread for him. Will he eat flowers?"

"He tried some on the way here," Alida said. "He likes apples."

Her mother smiled. "Good. I'm sure the root cellars hold something he will eat," she said.

Alida thanked her. "I was afraid you'd be angry at me for bringing him here."

Her mother's smile dimmed and she looked somber. "Others might be at first, but I am not. I'm grateful to him. I have waited for you every single day."

Alida stared at her mother. "You knew I was coming?"

Her mother shook her head. "No. But I hoped you would."

"Gavin let me out of the tower," Alida said, and began to explain.

Her mother listened, then put one finger on her lips, stopping her midword. "Ruth Oakes? I think I have heard that name."

Alida smiled. "She's a healer. Gavin's grandmother is staying with her now. She was sick, but Ruth helped her and—"

"This sounds like a long tale," Alida's mother interrupted.

Alida nodded. "It is."

"Wait for the feast so you don't have to tell it a hundred times," her mother said. "For now, go talk with your sister. She has missed you so much."

Alida glanced around. "But Gavin—"

"Look," her mother said, pointing.

Gavin was walking with her father, and they were laughing about something.

"I am trying to learn how Gavin does that," Alida said.

Her mother looked puzzled.

"Just the way he talks to everyone," Alida said. "He makes them happy, comfortable."

"Some humans have their own sort of magic," her mother said.

Alida nodded, then took a deep breath. "I have to tell you something," she said. Quietly, Alida explained how Holly had seen her wings. "But we were very careful not to leave any signs the guards could follow," she told her mother.

Then Alida looked up, expecting her mother to get angry.

But she didn't.

She just looked sad. "It is a terrible law that has harmed everyone. I can only hope young Lord Dunraven is a wiser man than his great-grandfather was."

"Maybe we could wish it?" Alida said.

Her mother shook her head. "That would be very dangerous magic," she said. "You will find another way."

Alida looked up, startled. "Me?"

Her mother nodded. "I hope so. That law has hurt everyone. Someone must correct old Lord Dunraven's mistakes—and my own. Now, go borrow a gown from your sister."

"A gown?" Alida echoed.

"For the feast," her mother said. "You need to look like Princess Alida tonight."

Chapter

9

The cooks worked hard all day.

So did everyone else.

By late afternoon the faerie lights were lit and floating in the air above the meadow.

Alida kept watching Terra.

She wanted to learn how to walk, to sit, to look as graceful as her sister and mother did.

Everyone had gotten dressed up.

Alida felt very strange wearing a gown of faerie silk. Her mother had braided tiny blue rosemary flowers into her hair. They smelled like pine trees after rain.

Gavin was too big to borrow clothes from any of the faeries.

But her father loaned him a hat with a long, curled feather.

When Gavin walked across the meadow, he looked out of place—too tall, no wings, almost clumsy, but handsome in a human way.

Alida saw some of the faeries staring at him, frowning.

Her mother made a point of talking with him where everyone could see. That helped, at least a little.

He sat with the faeries at the table nearest the flute players, smiling and eating everything that was brought to him.

Alida and her family sat at the biggest table, in the center of the meadow.

They always had.

When she was very young, Alida had never thought about why her family was always in the middle of things.

Now she knew why, but it was still odd to think that her mother was the queen. It was even odder to wonder who would be the next queen if Terra refused.

By evening the cooks had made clover pie and lilac soup and so many other wonderful things. And there was cheese and berry pudding for Gavin. Terra ate politely.

So did their mother and father.

Alida tried. She couldn't.

Even though she knew all the faeries were watching her, she couldn't help it.

The lilac soup was the color of the flowers, with bits of rose petals stirred in.

Even the spring rainwater had been chilled by magic.

Flowery frost patterns appeared on the glasses.

Alida ate and ate and then finally looked up.

Her mother glanced at her.

"Use your napkin," she said quietly.

Alida wiped her mouth, then apologized.

"Table manners are easy to learn," her mother said. "Was it terrible living in the castle?"

Alida told her about the stone chamber in the tower. And about the constant silence. Her mother shook her head.

"Old Lord Dunraven gave me his word that he would care for you," her mother said, "and that he would never bother any of us again." She lowered her head and her voice. "I was so afraid of him and his guards. I hope you can forgive me."

Alida touched her mother's hand. "I've seen the guards. I know why you were scared."

"Lord Dunraven will find out you are gone," Alida's mother said quietly, "sooner or later."

Alida set down her glass.

She didn't know what to say, except to apologize again for causing trouble.

"You didn't cause it," her mother said. "And I know you will help solve it."

"I will try," Alida promised.

"Stand up and tell us your tale," her mother said.

Alida looked out at all the faeries in the meadow. They were watching her, waiting. She hesitated. What if she stumbled over the words?

"I know," her mother said. "It is hard at first. It gets easier."

Alida stood up.

There was a little hissing sound as the faeries hushed one another.

Once they were quiet, Alida took a long breath.

"Don't leave anything out," her mother whispered.

"You all know that I was taken from my family . . . ," Alida began quietly, then realized that only the faeries at the big table could hear her.

She cleared her throat and started over.

"I was just beginning to learn to fly when I was taken away," she said, talking much louder. She had no idea what to say next. No one made a sound.

Whispers rose in the meadow.

Alida's mother lifted her right hand and there was silence.

Alida started over once more, and this time she managed to keep going.

She described the long, scary night in the wagon, galloping to Lord Dunraven's castle. She told them about the little stone room high in the tower, the human food that made her weak, the many years of silence.

She explained her escape with Gavin, and how his grandmother and her friend had become her friends. She told them everything.

When she was finished, she sat down.

"Gavin?" Alida's mother called out.

Alida could see how startled he was, but he stood up. "Yes, Your Majesty?"

Alida's mother shook her head. "Faerie queens are not like human noblemen. We use our names. Mine is Fiona."

"Yes, Fiona?" Gavin said instantly. Alida laughed with everyone else.

Gavin answered her mother's questions truthfully and quickly.

And when he was finished, everyone knew how much he cared about Alida and how happy he was to finally see magic, to know it was real.

"My grandmother never stopped telling the stories," he said before he sat down. "Many people have missed you very much."

The faeries were silent a moment, then they cheered.

But there were shouts mixed with the cheers—angry shouts.

"Humans only want our magic," a faerie with wide, lavender-colored wings called out. "They don't really care about us."

Someone began to argue with her. Voices rose until Alida couldn't understand what anyone was saying.

Her mother bent close to whisper. "This will not

be easy for any of us," she said. Then she stood up.

There was instant silence.

"Alida has come back to us, thanks to this human boy," she said. "We can argue tomorrow. Tonight we will rejoice that our princess is home at last!"

That brought a cheer that was pure and loud and glad.

"Music!" someone called out.

Terra ran to join the musicians.

Alida watched as they played. Terra's harp was much bigger than she was. Her flute shone silver in the faerie lights.

Alida and Gavin tried to do the faerie dances, but neither of them knew the steps, and they got in the way.

They ended up standing side by side watching the others dance, and Terra playing her harp with hundreds of strings.

"Whatever else happens," Alida said to Gavin, "I will be your sister every day that I live."

He bent to look into her eyes. "And I am your brother, Alida."

And for that one beautiful night, at least, there was nothing more to say.

Read on for more

The Faeries' Promise:

WISHES AND WINGS,

Book 3 in The Faeries' Promise series

Chapter

1

It was a chilly morning.

The faeries were lining up, getting ready to leave. Everyone was busy. Gavin was helping carry crates of food.

Alida was scared and excited all at once. It was wonderful to be back with her family after all the years she had spent alone, locked up in Lord Dunraven's castle.

It had eased her heart to tell her parents about the silent little room in the stone tower and about her friendship with Gavin. She told them how he had risked his life to help her escape—and that she freed him from Lord Dunraven's prison.

Her father said he was proud of her. Her mother hugged her and told her she was brave.

But Alida didn't feel brave.

Not now.

Her mother had decided it was time for them to return to the meadow near the human town of Ash Grove—which meant they would be breaking old Lord Dunraven's law.

Sooner or later his great-grandson would find out.

And Alida was afraid he would send his guards to find her.

The thought of even *seeing* the guards again scared Alida breathless. The idea of being taken back to Dunraven's castle terrified her.

Alida glanced at her mother.

She was walking fast, checking things, making sure the faeries were lining up, getting ready to begin the journey home.

Alida was glad her mother would be leading the

way. So was Gavin. They were both amazed at how well she had planned everything.

She had insisted that all the faeries wear clothing the color of oak leaves and grass and evening sky—so they would be harder to see in the forest shadows. She had even asked the weavers to make a brown shirt for Gavin.

It was easy to spot him near the end of the line, surrounded by her aunts and uncles. Eleven-year-old human boys were taller than faeries, even the grown-ups.

Alida looked into the faces around her. Almost everyone was smiling.

They had hated living so far from their home, and they all had long lists of things that they missed. Her Aunt Lily wasn't sure they should defy Dunraven's law by going home. But she agreed the berries here weren't as sweet as the ones in the woods near Ash Grove.

"Almost everyone seems happy to be going back," Alida said when her mother came to stand beside her. "Except Aunt Lily."

Her mother smiled. "My sister is opinionated, and she isn't the only one who thinks this might be dangerous. But it's time to go home. If we do, maybe one day the dragons and the unicorns will decide to come home too."

"Did I tell you I once saw unicorns from Lord Dunraven's tower?"

Her mother smiled again. "Yes, and it makes me very glad to know that. I was told they are all gone from the forests now."

"I wonder where the dragons are," Alida said.

"Don't worry," her mother said. "They're hiding somewhere, like the unicorns you saw. They have to be. There's hope."

Alida watched her mother walk back down the line again, stopping to talk to her sister, then bending low when a little blue-winged boy tugged at her sleeve. She wasn't dressed in a fancy gown this morning; she didn't look like a faerie queen. She looked like someone on her way to work in a garden.

Alida glanced at her father.

While her mother had been making decisions and listening to all the faeries' opinions, he had been busy too.

He had helped the weavers make magically strong harnesses for their goats.

The carpenters and wheelwrights had made stout little carts for them to pull.

Those carts were all lined up now, loaded with everything the faeries would need. Two of them were stacked with cheese and all the food from their root cellars. They had taken apart all their graceful wooden tables and packed them with care too.

Everyone's clothing—made of almost weightless faerie silk— had fit into three carts.

Their wooden plates and cups were heavy, though,

so they were stacked in strong willow baskets tied to the sides of the carts.

They had packed their precious glass jam jars too.

Alida remembered them from when she was little.

They had only thirty of them, a gift from a human farmer's wife long ago.

Alida saw her sister peering into one of the carts, checking her harp again.

All the faerie instruments had been wrapped in soft quilts, then packed very carefully.

Alida wished they could play music as they traveled.

They had played often while they were getting ready to leave. It had lifted everyone's heart and made the work go faster.

But once they started out, it wouldn't be safe.

Someone might hear the music.

Alida knew that her mother was right; some of the faeries were afraid to go home. She was too.

But her mother had explained her decision:

If Lord Dunraven was looking for them, he would almost certainly expect them to go deeper into the woods to hide.

He might think they would go as far as Lord Ermaedith's lands or even farther.

It made sense.

The last place he would expect them to go would be the meadow he knew about—the one their parents and grandparents and great- and great-great- and great-great-great-grandparents had lived in.

That meadow was barely a two-day walk from Ash Grove.

And Ash Grove was only a three day journey from Dunraven's castle.

Thinking about it like that made Alida feel cold and shaky.

Then she heard her mother's voice, clear and strong and pitched so everyone could hear. She turned.

"Parents will carry their babies," her mother was

saying. "Anyone who needs help will get it."

Alida watched her mother pause to see if anyone had a question before she went on.

"The elder faeries can take turns riding in the cart with benches. Our oldest children will be leading our six milk cows. We have brought flasks of rainwater. Use it sparingly, and we might not have to drink from streams."

When she finished, there were many questions. Once she had answered them, she looked at Alida's father.

He stepped forward. "Anyone who needs anything can ask me. I will walk last in line, to make sure no one gets lost or left behind."

Alida saw everyone nodding, getting used to the idea that they would be *walking*.

They all could have flown, of course.

They could have carried everything through the air, including the elders and the babies—even the goats and cows. But Lord Dunraven and his guards were always prowling, watching the roads and the sky. So the faeries would use mostly the narrow, hidden paths the deer and the wolves used.

The cows and goats could graze along the way. The faeries would be able to pick wildflowers to eat.

They would all be careful and quiet and make sure no one saw them.

Gavin had offered to walk ahead of them where they were most likely to see humans. Alida watched him. He was smiling, nodding at something someone had said.

She was so glad he had helped her find her family and that he had stayed to help them go home, to the meadow near Ash Grove.

Gavin's grandmother lived in Ash Grove.

Her name was Molly Hamilton, and she had moved in with her oldest friend, Ruth Oakes. They were both kind and brave.

Alida was grateful to them, too.

They had known she was a faerie.

But they had let her stay with them while she was learning to fly and figuring out how to help Gavin escape from Lord Dunraven's castle.

They both had white hair—they were old enough to remember faeries.

Alida stood up a little straighter, thinking about Ruth and Molly. They were both very brave. They hadn't been afraid to help her, no matter what old Lord Dunraven's law said. If she and Gavin were very careful, maybe they would be able to visit each other.

"Are you all ready to begin the journey?" Alida's mother called out. Her voice was clear and strong.

"Yes!" the faeries shouted.

Most of them, anyway.

Now that the time had come, the ones who weren't sure were grumbling. One of Alida's oldest uncles was frowning. But when Alida's mother began to walk, everyone followed.

Chapter
2

At first Alida's mother walked at a slow, steady pace, glancing back again and again.

Once everyone was moving steadily through the trees, Alida went to walk beside her.

"Are you all right?" her mother asked.

"I'm a little scared," Alida said. "Why would old Lord Dunraven make such a terrible law?"

Her mother shrugged. "Your aunt Clare always says he thought daydreaming and storytelling wasted time that would be better spent working. But humans and faeries are alike when it comes to that. Without stories and a little magic, we aren't happy."

Alida nodded. "The day I walked through Ash

Grove, I tied my shawl tight over my wings. I was trying so hard to look like a human girl. At first I thought someone might ask if I needed help. But no one did. They all looked tired and angry."

"The human farmers always had to give part of their crops to the Dunravens," her mother said. "We used to see the big, creaking wagons carrying off barley, wheat, oats, field crops of every kind—even cheese and eggs—all to feed the guards. I'm sure it's even worse now."

Alida nodded. It probably was.

Lord Dunraven had hundreds of guards now.

Alida walked in silence for a while, thinking about old Lord Dunraven, and his sons and grandsons and great-grandsons.

It all seemed so unfair.

"Before the law," her mother said quietly, "Lord Dunraven's guards would ride through the forests sometimes. But there weren't many of them, and the faeries weren't afraid of them."

That was hard for Alida to imagine.

Everyone was afraid of the guards now.

"When I was your age," her mother said, "there were guards visiting us when a flight of dragons flew over. We all stood there, humans and faeries, amazed by how beautiful they were."

"Are they dangerous?" Alida asked.

Her mother glanced at her. "The guards? Not then. They are now."

Alida shook her head. "I meant the dragons."

"Very dangerous," her mother said. "But only if something bothers them or scares them."

"And the unicorns?" Alida asked.

Her mother smiled. "Unicorns are kind and shy. I have never understood why Old Lord Dunraven would hunt them."

"How many Lord Dunravens have there been?" Alida asked.

Her mother glanced at the carts before she answered. "Twenty or more? I don't know. Some were much better than others." She leaned close to kiss Alida on the forehead. "But there have been more than a thousand faerie queens. And I am coming to believe that you will be the next one. Just keep walking," she said. "I'll hurry."

Then she spread her wings and flew, very low, all the way to the end of the line, where Gavin was helping one of her aunts lift something into a cart while it rolled along. Alida's sister, Terra, was carrying a baby, and she was smiling. If she was scared, it didn't show.

Alida kept her pace the same, thinking about what her mother had said. It felt very odd to be the one leading the way. She kept glancing back at her parents, her family, all her relatives and friends. She was so grateful to be with them again. Gavin, his grandmother Molly, Ruth Oakes—and John the stableman who had been the one to take her to Lord Dunraven's castle—they had all helped to free her.

"Some of the elders are having a hard time keeping up," her mother said when she came back.

"Your aunt Lily is complaining already."

Alida nodded to be polite, then she made sure no one was close. "I have a question," she said quietly.

Her mother looked at her. "Yes?"

"There's a man named John at Lord Dunraven's castle," Alida began. "He was old when he took me there, and he looked the same when he helped me escape. Can humans live that long?"

"No," Alida's mother said. "But John is not human."

"But he doesn't have wings, and he—"

"He gave up his wings," her mother said. "In order to stay at the castle, to make sure you were not hurt."

Alida stared at her mother. "He's a faerie?"

"Yes."

Alida was astonished. John looked like any human.

"He wished his wings away," her mother said. "And he wished himself taller. He's very good with horses, so he found work in the castle stable. He did it for me. To keep an eye on you."

Alida looked up at her mother.

Her mother sighed. "John used big, dangerous magic to make himself look human. I don't think he could get his wings back now."

Alida couldn't imagine not having wings.

Her mother touched her cheek. "John is clever. Most of the castle positions are passed from father to son, and the Dunravens never set foot in the barn. So he is safe. He hires the stablemen, and he makes sure none stays long enough to wonder how old he is."

Alida's heart was heavy. When she looked up, her mother was watching her.

"Being the queen is not easy," she said, "but it has to be done."

The Unicorn's Secret

Read the books that started it all!

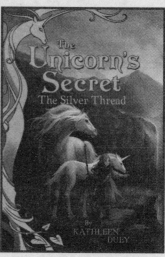